Lunar Caustic

Lunar Caustic

Malcolm Lowry

Edited by Earle Birney
and Margerie Lowry
With a Foreword
by Conrad Knickerbocker

JONATHAN CAPE
THIRTY BEDFORD SQUARE   LONDON

First published in the *Paris Review*, No. 29, 1963
© 1963 by Margerie Lowry
Reissued 1968 in Jonathan Cape Editions
Reprinted 1971
Reissued 1977 in this format

Jonathan Cape Ltd, 30 Bedford Square, London WC1

ISBN 0 224 01346 7

The article by Conrad Knickerbocker,
'Malcolm Lowry and the Outer Circle of Hell',
is reprinted by permission of
Russell & Volkening Inc.

Printed in Great Britain by litho at The Anchor Press Ltd
and bound by Wm Brendon & Son Ltd
both of Tiptree, Essex

Malcolm Lowry and the Outer Circle of Hell

The themes of *Lunar Caustic*, like unreliable demons, pursued Malcolm Lowry for most of his writing life. He first undertook the story in 1934, during his particularly black discovery of New York in his youth. The city, he once wrote a friend, 'favours brief and furious outbursts, but not the long haul. Moreover for all its drama and existential fury, or perhaps because of it, it's a city where it can be remarkably hard – or so it seems to me – to get on the right side of one's despair ...'

Lowry's encounter with New York was almost entirely in terms of loss, of departures and the beginning of long voyages. He was already, at the age of twenty-seven, a veteran seafarer (he had shipped around the world as a bosun's boy on a tramp steamer before taking an English tripos at Cambridge). Behind were a first novel, *Ultramarine*, and a broken marriage. He carried little else with him besides the horrendously developed sense of the 'drunken madly revolving world' that was to receive such intense expression in *Under the Volcano*.

On his arrival from France, when asked by a New York customs officer if he had anything to declare, he replied, 'I don't know. Let's see.' They opened his large trunk. It contained one football boot and a copy of *Moby Dick*. Existing on a small income from his well-to-do cottonbroker father, for the next year he lived in a near-slum, communicated with almost no one, drank and wrote. He always insisted that his stay in Bellevue Hospital during that time was voluntary, a 'deliberate pilgrimage' to gather material. Towards the end of this period he completed the first draft of what was eventually to be *Lunar Caustic*.

He took the manuscript with him on his subsequent journey to Hollywood and continued to work on the story sporadically, first in Cuernavaca, later in British Columbia and finally in England, for the next twenty-two years.

Lowry would have placed the present version in the category of work-in-progress, although two complete manuscripts and a partially finished third draft, plus a mass of notes, existed at the time of his sudden death by accidental suffocation in the tiny Sussex village of Ripe in 1957. He was a brooding, relentless, almost pathologically dissatisfied reviser of his own writing. At one point in the mid-1930s, an early draft, under the title *The Last Address*, was accepted by Whit Burnett for *Story* magazine, but Lowry called it back. He permitted a French translation of the first version (it appeared in *L'Esprit* in 1956) only because, he explained, he was afraid of losing the manuscripts, something that had happened to him more than once. The author, although admitting the French version 'has an air of completion', declared that he would have to put in at least six more months of solid work on it before he could offer it as finished.

In England during his last years, Lowry had decided to do another draft of *Lunar Caustic*, this time as a novella, to get the feel of it before undertaking it as a novel. At the time of his death he had reassembled and mixed the two drafts in the working method he always used. He often had five, ten or even twenty versions of a sentence, paragraph or chapter going at once. From these, he selected the best, blending, annealing and reworking again and again to obtain the highly charged, multi-levelled style that characterizes his best writing.

Lunar Caustic was to have been a major segment in *The Voyage That Never Ends*, a sequence of seven novels that Lowry planned round the central work, *Under the Volcano*. He saw the projected cycle as a modern *Divine Comedy*, with the ultimate goal Hell and redemption. *Lunar Caustic*, he once said, was only Purgatory. Yet he conceived of its characters as 'the caryatids of human anguish' that hold up the world from below, and for the protagonist, William Plantagenet, the sound of the hospital door closing behind him 'with a dithering crack' is the true sound of a damnation as immense and terrible as the City itself.

CONRAD KNICKERBOCKER

The editors, Lowry's second wife and Earle Birney, an old friend and neighbour of the author and professor of English at the University of British Columbia, describe the present version as being primarily a job of splicing, in an approximation of Lowry's method and intent. 'We have not added a line,' Mrs Lowry has said in a letter to me. 'Malcolm, of course, would then have rewritten, but who could do it as he would have?'

C. K.

I

A man leaves a dockside tavern in the early morning, the smell of the sea in his nostrils, and a whisky bottle in his pocket, gliding over the cobbles lightly as a ship leaving harbour.

Soon he is running into a storm and tacking from side to side, frantically trying to get back. Now he will go into any harbour at all.

He goes into another saloon.

From this he emerges, cunningly repaired; but he is in difficulties once more. This time it is serious: he is nearly run over by a street car, he bangs his head on a wall, once he falls over an ashcan where he has thrown a bottle. Passers-by stare at him curiously, some with anger, others with amusement, or even a strange avidity.

This time he seeks refuge up an alley, and leans against the wall in an attitude of dejection, as if trying to remember something.

Again the pilgrimage starts but his course is so erratic it seems he must be looking for, rather than trying to remember something. Or perhaps, like the poor cat who had lost an eye in a battle, he is just looking for his sight?

The heat rises up from the pavements, a mighty force, New York groans and roars above, around, below him: white birds flash in the quivering air, a bridge strides over the river. Signs nod past him: *The Best for Less, Romeo and Juliet, the greatest love story in the world, No Cover at Any Time, When pain threatens, strikes –*

He enters another tavern, where presently he is talking of people he had never known, of places he had never been. Through the open door he is aware of the hospital, towering up above the river. Near him arrogant bearded derelicts cringe over spittoons, and of these men he seems afraid. Sweat floods his face. From the depths of the tavern comes a sound of moaning, and a sound of ticking.

Outside, again the pilgrimage starts, he wanders from saloon to saloon as though searching for something, but always keeping the hospital in sight, as if the saloons were only points on his circumference. In a street along the waterfront, where a bell is clanging, he halts; a terrible old woman, whose black veil only partly conceals her ravaged face, is trying to post a letter, trying repeatedly and failing, but posting it finally, with shaking hands that are not like hands at all.

A strange notion strikes him : the letter is for him. He takes a drink from his bottle.

In the Elevated a heavenly wind is blowing and there is a view of the river, but he is walking as though stepping over obstacles, or like Ahab stumbling from side to side on the careening bridge, 'feeling that he encompassed in his stare oceans from which might be revealed that phantom destroyer of himself.'

Down in the street the heat is terrific. Tabloid headlines : *Thousands collapse in Heat Wave. Hundreds Dead. Roosevelt Raps Warmongers. Civil War in Spain.*

Once he stops in a church, his lips moving in something like a prayer. Inside it is cool : around the walls are pictured the stages of the cross. Nobody seems to be looking. He likes drinking in churches particularly.

But afterwards he comes to a place not like a church at all.

This is the hospital: all day he has hovered round it; now it looms up closer than ever. This is his objective. Tilting the bottle to his mouth he takes a long, final draught: drops run down his neck, mingling with the sweat.

'I want to hear the song of the Negroes,' he roars. '*Veut-on que je disparaisse, que je plonge, à la recherche de l'anneau* ... I am sent to save my father, to find my son, to heal the eternal horror of three, to resolve the immedicable horror of opposites!'

With the dithering crack of a ship going on the rocks the door shuts behind him.

II

Looking down from the high buildings on 4th or 5th Avenue and 30th Street in New York you would never have thought there was grass growing down to the East River. But between the Observation Ward of the Psychiatric Hospital and the water, in a little lot to the left of the powerhouse – a building distinguishable even from midtown because its derricks are out of alignment and yearn over towards the hospital – you might have seen this grass as it grew there.

At the edge of the grass was a broken coal barge and beyond that, a little harbour bounded by two wharves. On the wharf to the right was the powerhouse and in front of it a shed used by the doctors as a garage, near which a green hospital ambulance was often parked.

The wharf to the left, though complicated by an extraordinary arrangement of wind-chutes, foghorns and ventilators, whose purpose was undiscoverable, had nevertheless a friendlier, more simple quality of holiday, of the seaside. Here white and blue motor boats were moored, with such names as 'Empty Pockets III', 'Dunwoiken', 'Lovebird', boats which seemed as they nudged and nibbled ceaselessly at the suicidal blackness of the stream to tell tender tales of girls in summer.

The only boat that tied up to the wharf by the powerhouse was the ferry, Tekanas. This, so someone said, went to the Ice Palace at Rockaway.

But between the two wharves and fast against the poverty grass before the hospital lay the coal barge, sunken, abandoned, open, hull cracked, bollards adrift, tiller smashed, its hold still choked with coal dust, silt, and earth through which emerald shoots had sprouted.

In the evenings, the patients would stare out over the river at the Jack Frost Sugar Works, and if there was a ship unloading there it seemed to them she might have some special news for them, bringing deliverance. But none ever came ...

Sometimes, when there was a mist, river and sky merged in a white calm through which little masts and tilted, squat towers seemed to be slowly flying. A smudged gasworks crouched like something that could spring, behind the leaning, vaporous geometry of cranes and angled church steeples; and the factory chimneys waved endless handkerchiefs of smoke.

Farewell, farewell, life!

Every so often, when a ship passed, there would be a curious mass movement towards the barred windows, a surging whose source was in the breasts of the mad seamen and firemen there, but to which all were tributary: even those whose heads had been bowed for days rose at this stirring, their bodies shaking as though roused suddenly from nightmare or from the dead, while their lips would burst with a sound, partly a cheer and partly a wailing shriek, like some cry of the imprisoned spirit of New York itself, that spirit haunting the abyss between Europe and America and brooding like futurity over the Western Ocean. The eyes of all would watch the ship with a strange, hungry supplication.

But more often when a ship went by or backed out from the docks opposite and swung around to steam towards the open sea, there was a dead silence in the ward and a strange foreboding as though all hope were sailing with the tide.

III

The man who now gave the name of Bill Plantagenet, but who had first announced himself as the s.s. *Lawhill*, awoke certain at least that he was on a ship. If not, where did those isolated clangings come from, those sounds of iron on iron? He recognized the crunch of water pouring over the scuttle, the heavy tramp of feet on the deck above, the steady Frère *Jacques*: *Frère Jacques* of the engines. He was on a ship, taking him back to England, which he never should have left in the first place. Now he was conscious of his racked, trembling, malodorous body. Daylight sent probes of agony against his eyelids. Opening them, he saw three

Negro sailors vigorously washing down the deck. He shut his eyes again. Impossible, he thought.

And if he were on a ship, and supposedly therefore in the fo'c'sle, the alleyway at the end of which his bunk was must be taking up the fo'c'sle's entire length. He considered this madness – then the thrumming became so loud in his ears he found himself wondering if he were not lying in the propeller shaft.

As day grew, the noise became more ghastly: what sounded like a railway seemed to be running just over the ceiling. Another night came. The noise grew worse and, stranger yet, the crew kept multiplying. More and more men, bruised, wounded, and always drunk, were hurled down the alley by petty officers to lie face downward, screaming, or suddenly asleep on their hard bunks.

He was awake. What had he done last night? Played the piano? Was it last night? Nothing at all, perhaps, yet remorse tore at his vitals. He needed a drink desperately. He did not know whether his eyes were closed or open. Horrid shapes plunged out of the blankness, gibbering, rubbing their bristles against his face, but he couldn't move. Something had got under his bed too, a bear that kept trying to get up. Voices, a prosopopoeia of voices, murmured in his ears, ebbed away, murmured again, cackled, shrieked, cajoled; voices pleading with him to stop drinking, to die and be damned. Thronged, dreadful shadows came close, were snatched away. A cataract of water was pouring through the wall, filling the room. A red hand gesticulated, prodded him: over a ravaged mountain side a swift stream was carrying with it legless bodies yelling out of great eye-sockets, in which were broken teeth. Music mounted to a screech, subsided. On a tumbled bloodstained bed in a house whose face was

The monkey axed the baboon, shoot a game of
   pool?
That ole monkey – '

'Get back to your room, Battle!' an attendant shouted, and Battle vanished.

What time was it, Plantagenet wondered? What *day* was it? ...

Mr Kalowsky looked small and melancholy in bed. 'We can only wait and see,' he said, pursing his lips in and out. 'So many things can happen in a lifetime ... I am eighty-two years, and my father lose his money – that's one thing. I hike from Berlin to Paris, that's another.

'I was one little Jew and my father became rich in Memel, Lithuania. From there he moved to Königsberg and from there to Berlin. In Berlin I served my time as a silversmith. Then I roamed around.

'I hiked from Berlin to Paris. A rich woman paid my fare the first time but the second time the Germans went to war – 1870. Anyone who couldn't speak fluently French was a Prussian. So I walked over the Jura mountains ...'

The lights went out.

Battle, luminous in white pyjamas, was tap-dancing in the dark, his white teeth gleaming as he soft-shoed, whispering :

'That ole monkey put the ace in the corner and deuce
   at the side
Say, Hightop, give the ace a ride!
The monkey broke the ball, made the 8, 9, 10,
Put deep bottom on a cue ball and kicked the fifteen
   in! ...'

IV

Sweltering, delirious night telescoped into foetid day: day into night : he realized it was twilight though he had thought it dawn. Someone sat on his bed with a hand on his pulse, and forcing his eyes open he saw a wavering white form which divided into three, became two and finally came into focus as a man in a white gown.

The man – a doctor? – dropped Plantagenet's wrist. 'You've certainly got the shakes,' he said.

'Shakes, yes.' The quivering of his body was such that, after his initial surprise, it impeded his speech, 'Well, what's wrong with me?' He tried to rise on his elbow which, jumping, did not hold him; he sank or fell back with a groan.

'Alcohol ... And perhaps other things. Judging from your remarks in the last few days I'd say it's about as bad as you suspect.'

'What did I say?'

The doctor smiled slightly. 'You said, "Hullo, father, return to the presexual revives the necessity for nutrition." Sounds as though you once read a little book.'

'Oh Christ! Oh God! Oh Jesus!'

'You made some fine giveaways.' The doctor shook his head. 'But let's be concrete. Who is Ruth? And the six Cantabs?'

'Bill Plantagenet and his Seven Hot Cantabs,' he corrected and continued with nervous rapidity, 'We went a treat in Cambridge, at the May Balls, or at the Footlights Club. We were all right with our first records, too, we took that seriously. But when we got over here we just broke up.' He grasped the doctor's living in the pre-existence of some unimaginable catastrophe, and he steadied himself a moment against the sill, feeling the doomed earth itself stagger in its heaving spastic flight towards the Hercules Butterfly.

'I'se bin here just up to almos' exactly let me see, men, seventeen days and a half exac.' Battle was tap-dancing behind him.

'Dat guy talks wif his feet.'

'Yes sah,' said Battle, whirling around, 'I do that thing, man!'

'He comes from Louisiana; he knocked that old engineer's tooth out,' said Garry beside him.

'Now I catch Jersey Blues,' Battle said. 'I'se got fifteen customers.' He skipped off.

— He was conscious that time was passing, that he was getting 'better'. The periodic, shuddering metamorphoses his mind projected upon almost every object, bad as they were, were no longer so atrociously vivid. Moreover he had at first forgotten for long periods that he was able to get out when he wished. Now he forgot more rarely. He was only a drunk, he thought. Though he had pretended for a while that he was not, that he was mad with the full dignity of madness. The man who thought himself a ship. And time was passing; only his sense of it had become subject to a curious prorogation. He didn't know whether it was the fifth or the sixth day that found him still staring out of the window at twilight, with Garry and Mr Kalowsky by his side like old faithful friends. The powerhouse no longer was a foreign place. The wharves, the motor boats, the poverty grass, he had received into his mind now, together with the old coal barge, to which Garry often turned.

'It was condemned,' he would say. 'One day it collapsed and fell apart.'

Garry looked at Bill wildly, grasping his arm. 'The houses of Pompeii were fallen!' His voice dropped to a whisper. 'And you'd see a house suddenly fall in, *collapse*; and the melted rock and the hot mud poured down; people ran down to the boat. But it was collapsed.' Looking up he added breathlessly, 'Gold rings and boxes of money and strange tables and they dug down the side of the great mountain.'

'Yes suh, man,' Battle danced. 'He's de ole man of the mountain. He track along wit a horse and ban'. Put a jiggle in his tail as you pass him by – ' he danced away singing, 'De biggest turtle I ever see, he twice de size of you and me.'

Kalowsky stood quietly watching, pursing his lips continually in and out like a dying fish. What was that film Plantagenet had seen once, where the shark went on swallowing the live fish, even after it was dead?

Garry clutched Bill's arm again. 'Listen. What do you think will be left of this building in a few years? *I'll* tell you. They'd still find the brick buildings but there wouldn't be any beds, only a rusty frame, and the radiator, you would touch it and it would fall to pieces. All that would be left of the piano would be the keys; all the rest would rot. And the floor.' Garry paused, considering. 'And one of us sat on it and the whole thing fell down, collapsed. We went out the door where the fire escape was and it fell off, seven storeys off, it fell down.'

But what had really begun to make things a bit more tolerable for him was this very comradeship of his two friends. Sometimes he even tricked himself into imagining that a kind of purpose united them. Part of the truth was that, like new boys in a hostile school, like sailors on their first long voyage on a miserable ship, like soldiers in a prison camp, they were drawn together in a doleful world where their daydreams mingled, and finding expression, jostled irresponsibly, yet with an underlying irreducible logic, around the subject of homecoming. Yet with them 'home' was never mentioned, save very obliquely by Garry. Plantagenet sometimes suspected the true nature of that miraculous day they looked to when their troubles would all be ended, but he couldn't give it away. Meanwhile it masqueraded before them in the hues of various dawns – never mind what was going to happen in its practical noontide.

As a matter of fact, with one part of his mind, he was seriously convinced that Mr Kalowsky and Garry were at least as sane as he : he felt too that he would be able to convince the doctor, when he saw him again, that an injustice had been committed, which never would otherwise have come to light.

But trying to explain their whole situation to himself his mind seemed to flicker senselessly between extremities of insincerities. For with another part of his mind he felt the encroachment of a chilling fear, eclipsing all other feelings, that the thing they wanted was coming for him alone, before he was ready for it; it was a fear worse than the fear that when money was low one would have to stop drinking; it was compounded of harrowed longing and hatred, of fathomless compunctions, and of a paradoxical remorse, as it were in advance, for his failure to attempt finally something he was not now going to have time for, to face the world honestly; it was the shadow of a city of dreadful night without splendour that fell on his soul; and how darkly it fell whenever a ship passed !

V

Pneumatic Tube Station 382; Electro-cardiograph dept. 257; Operating Rooms 217; Physiotherapy 320; Neuro. Path. Laboratory 204; Dial O for Psychiatric numbers ...

Occupational Therapy Dept. 338 ...

The room was filled by an almost continual unebbing surf of noise. Unable to stand it at first, Plantagenet had ended by so loudly hammering the soft metal into a fluted ashtray that it seemed he wished to drown out this bane of noise for ever.

But there were quieter occupations. Beside him, Garry was painting a wooden duck green, and Battle was plaiting with straw a cymbal-shaped hat, and singing 'Ole Man Mose Is Dead', though this therapy always brought on his fits, and back in the ward again it was certain he would try to get up the chimney.

'Well, how are you, Battle?' An attendant glanced at the group, paused long enough to jingle his huge keys, then passed on. Bill heard voices from up the ward muttering, 'Is this a hospital or a prison?' 'It's a prison.' 'Well, I have to come down here once a week, mister ... Anything more, I draw on interest.' 'That guy asleep over there, see? He had two guns in his pocket, two twenty-twos and a suitcase plenty full of bullets. Held up that store, you know.'

'It fell apart, collapsed!'

'Well, I don't know exac'ly wen dey gonna let me out,' Battle murmured vacantly. 'I axed de doctah but he don' say yet, but I guess it gonna be soon.'

'After you've taken yo' temp'rature.'

'De ole lollipop, yes sah, man!' said Battle. 'When

dey come an' give you de lollipop den you go an' play de piano, sho.' He shuffled round a corner.

'Come on. I'll teach you semaphore.' Garry said. In a moment Battle was signalling in imitation.

'Move yo' lef han' to E. To make M, move to F,' Battle repeated after Garry, then immediately he started to shadow-box again, though Garry went on signalling. A little man with a beard passing by said to himself loudly, 'That's semaphore. All Boy Scouts use it.'

Battle snorted and returned to semaphore, to the delight of Garry, shouting, 'Ayeh! Beah! Gee!' while Garry shifted his pink-palmed paws for him. Two other Negroes appeared now as the semaphoring was being transformed into a grotesque dance. 'Doo, tee, da, do,' they shouted, pouncing around the beds. 'Tee, da, do, aw-aw, do pup depup, da woo!'

Battle was hitting Garry playfully. 'See dat lef' jab! Is yo' scared of me?'

Plantagenet suddenly caught sight, through the bars, of four operations being performed simultaneously in the wing opposite in high sunlit rooms of glass, so that it seemed as though the front of that part of the hospital had suddenly become *open*, revealing, as in the cabin plans of the 'Cunard' or in charts of the human anatomy itself, the activities behind the wraith of iron or brick or shin : and it was strange to watch these white-masked figures working behind the glass that now glittered like a mirage. At the same time the whole scene that lay before them suddenly, like the looming swift white hand of a traffic policeman, reeled towards him; he felt he had only to stretch out his fingers to touch the doctor working on the right side of the table sewing up the incision, or the nurse plastering and binding the patient or placing the blanket over the body; and it seemed to him that all these dressings and redressings in these hours of north light were at the same time being placed, torn away and replaced, on a laceration of his own mind.

Or – was he dead? Ah ha, watch the surgeon slit the foot of the dead man! What next, Nostradamus? Will blood appear? Or has it clotted, in some vital organ? Bleed, dead man, bleed, set the poor surgeon's mind at rest, so that he won't have to get drunk and go through the jumps and the blind staggers; the horror of the rats, the wheeling bushmills, and the Orange Bitters; bleed, so that he won't find himself reflecting in summer that even Nature herself is shot through with jitteriness, the neurotic squirrel and the sparrows nibbling the dung where the octoroons, the creole and the quadroon have galloped past in black dust; bleed, so that he will not have to think how much more beautiful women are when you are dying, and they sway down the streets under the fainting trees, their bosoms tossing like blossoms in the warm gusts; bleed, so that he will not have to hear the louse of conscience, nor the groaning of imaginary men, nor see, on the window blind all night the bad ghosts –

'But Mr Battle, you're taking the hat all to pieces. You're doing it all wrong,' a schoolteacherly voice was saying.

'Ah'm doin' it all wrong, am I Ma'm? To ma' way of thinkin' Ah'm doin' it O.K. Is dis treatment 29 or what?' And a moment later, as the gaily coloured hat was being torn to pieces, 'Ah'll give yuh treatment 63!'

Later, when the nine high candles in their circular base were lighted above the old men who were considered too jittery or too obscene to eat with the others in the regular room, and they were bent over

26

their stew in a grey, trembling despair, some seeming not to know they were eating at all, the food perhaps tasteless to them as they cuffed it slowly and sleepily with their harmless spoons, others not even attempting to eat but wearing a fixed smile, as though the thought even of misery afforded them some perverse comfort, Plantagenet, watching them, gradually thought he understood the meaning of death, not as a sudden dispatch of violence, but as a function of life. He stood up, as if to strike off an enemy, then let his hands drop limply to his sides.

There was a huge clanking of keys, the bathroom door was being unlocked, and Battle, blundering around just then, shouted 'Toilet! Toilet! Ah don' feel like sittin' down. Ah just feel like shittin' on de flo'.' 'Time for a butt,' a voice murmured and the shuffling sounded quicker.

The door of the bathroom clanged shut and the keys went clinking down the corridor.

When they got back to the main ward Battle was trying to climb up the chimney. The attendants pulled him down and he fell flat on his face, refusing to move.

Garry and Bill stood near. Mr Kalowsky was watching them, his spoon poised, his gaze passing mechanically, like a slowed fan, from them to Battle and to the attendants and back again.

After a while the heroic Battle stirred and, sitting up, rubbed his head and remarked with consummate sanity, looking full at the nurse:

'No matter what a woman play, whether she know or whether she don' know, she beat you at it.'

One of the hottest days of all was the day of the puppet show. The three friends made their beds early.

'I don't say this to many people,' Garry was saying to Mr Kalowsky as he smoothed down the grimed sheets, 'but I wish you were my father.'

Keys clashed like cymbals, the bathroom door banged open, the daily routine was beginning. Presently the rooms were filled with the dreadful noise of shuffling feet. Heads bowed, the patients scraped their cord soles along the floor, save when they were called to the lavatory or for a smoke. For a minute or two after that they held themselves erect as if they had forgotten the horror of their lives, but soon one head bowed down again, then another, while their senses, that had almost thrilled to life again in that momentary, trembling order, became numbed, unaware of their foreheads gleaming with sweat or their dirty feet and bodies. Occasionally when some one sat down on his bed, an attendant shouted.

'Get up there! Keep moving!'

Then he would take his place once more in the procession which Garry, Plantagenet and Mr Kalowsky had long since joined.

'I am just the Wandering Jew,' Mr Kalowsky said with a wry smile. 'It was in 1870,' he added, 'and the Germans went to war.' They were passing the tall barred window which gave on the east side of the hospital, round which the sunlight seemed to be racing like a small vicious boy, he thought, bursting with health and din, tormenting them. 'That evening it was sunset and the French peasants came from work. I had a cane in my hand with a big piece of iron in the end

'After you've seen the doctor, I'll tell you, you'll take us to Elengland. Mr Kalowsky and I and maybe my brother; I can see it all plainly. There are some farms there. I know I might see artists on the hillside or cows and sheep grazing in green pastures. I can see them there, the artists, painting pictures of flowers and the different birds and the mountains and the lakes and trees. Or,' he dropped his voice, 'you might go to one part where an artist is painting pictures of ruins.'

In the ward a game of ping-pong had been instituted between Battle and the nurse, but Battle was already firmly taking down the net, the ball a red bubble in his mouth: 'Dis ain't no bean parlour, nor yet no tennis parlour,' he complained and a moment later, when they had reached the tall window, he overtook them, dancing and singing: 'I was goin' down Main. I met a police. He ask ma name. Battle, Ah said. And around ma arm was a bracelet chain – '

They had come round to the ward facing the East River again. 'Do you see that old coal barge?' asked Garry. 'I can tell you about her. Yes sir, I can tell them ... In 1914 she was loaded with fine coal, but the rope snapped, she drifted with the current, and most of the coal is all at the bottom now. The rest is buried here and the barge is smashed, broken.'

'Now Garry, tell us a humoristic story,' said Mr Kalowsky with a kindly look at both of them.

'Sure,' said Garry, and their step became a little brisker. 'Over in India in the jungles there was a mother and a baby elephant. The natives wanted to trap the baby elephant and bring him back alive. The mother elephant and the baby were out one day in the jungles and the baby was chasing a butterfly and fell in the pit and the white men tied her up –'

Then it was time for the puppet show. The patients took their places slowly, plucking the cotton thread out of each other's gowns, made of towelling.

'Stop pulling things off me! What you think you're doing?'

'Going to hit me?'

'I ain't going to hit you.'

'Quiet, boys, please! Quiet now.'

'I hit you two time. I hit you one there and one there.'

'Jesus Christ up in the sky, look up dar, Ah can see him : Abraham Lincoln down under de flo' – but whar George Washington? dat's what I want to know – Let no one take ma seat while Ah'm gone,' Battle danced out of the room and returned swiftly with a tabloid newspaper.

Plantagenet looked over his shoulder and read :

TWO SNAKES WRITHE IN COURT
WOMEN QUAKE AS REPTILES SPIT VENOM AT TRIAL

Buzzing their hollow rattles so loud that women in the far corners of the crowded courtroom shivered at the frightening sounds, two diamond-backed rattlesnakes, glittering in their new skins, today were placed on the council table in Superior Judge Fricke's court, where Robert S. James, Birmingham barber, crouched ghost-faced and jittery at his trial for the murder of his golden-haired bride –

He noted the date line with a flash of terror. That long!

Garry read with difficulty: *'Vice Queen back from cell to reign in Atlantic City.'*

'Jesus, those old snakes,' said somebody. 'Have you ever had those old snakes?'

'The wheels. They're worse. Who'll cure a man of the wheels?'

'What's the matter with your head that you read all these lies?' said Mr Kalowsky. 'And all this dirt.'

'Suppose I tried to tell the doctor I thought you'd been framed, Mr Kalowsky,' Plantagenet said, almost to himself. 'You're as sane as most people I know. Trouble is: am I? And would he listen to me?'

'Two snakes – in court – at trial.' Garry was spelling out. 'Gee whiz!'

'Jesus, I know a guy on the *News*, and when I get out of here I'm going up there and tell him what I think of this goddam place. Now Jesus, listen to this, will you? I was sitting on the wharf drinking whisky when this cop came up and said, "What are you doing?" I said, "Why, man, I'm just drinking this pint of whisky and now I think I'll finish it." Well, he watched me finish it and the next thing I knew I was being taken here. Why, I was in complete control of myself. I had eighteen toothpicks, I knew exactly – see – and I told this cop so, and I used one of them, for Christ sake ... That makes nineteen toothpicks I've got waiting for me downstairs and I'll get them when I go, goddam if I won't. And they say I'm crazy!'

There was a roar in the building, shaking the doors. 'See dat plane comin' down?' said Battle. 'That's no plane, that's an automobile.' 'An automobile can't fly.' 'Yes sir, that's an automobile *can* fly. Let no one jump off after women now!' Battle yelled, leaping to his feet.

'Hullo,' said a voice in Plantagenet's ear. 'How's Mr Remorse today?'

'Oh, hullo, Doctor,' he said, half rising. 'Not bad. Fine. I've quite a lot to tell you, if you have time one day.'

'I see by your chart you've been coming along all right.' The doctor sat down beside him heavily. 'I meant to see you before this,' he said, 'but I've never been so busy ... and the heat ... What's on your mind?'

'Oh – never mind now. I'll come to your office, if I may?' The doctor nodded, absently. 'Well,' Plantagenet added nervously, 'what about this puppet show?'

'Mmm. My idea, mostly. It represents a definitely socializing influence, giving the patients an opportunity to get together and control their usual tendencies for emotional outbursts.' He glanced around, frowning thoughtfully. 'Then too, the patients have a common experience which they can share later, and talk about. It is sometimes moderately successful.'

At one end of the wardroom table a wooden rectangular construction had appeared, with an oblong slit for the stage, covered by green and yellow curtains, against which leaned the puppeteer, a sane man from 'outside', arms akimbo, face ochre from a dark lantern. 'There's been some mixup with your music,' he said. 'Music next week. You remember,' he added with a little laugh, 'Caspar bought himself a balloon, and we shall see what adventures he will have.'

'Yes sah!'

'All right, here we go.' The puppeteer drew down the blind on the window nearest to him, creating an illusion of coolness, though the room was by no means dark.

34

'Yes sah boss,' said Battle, scratching himself. 'Ready for sho'.'

The curtains disclosed that Caspar was Punch, and that Punch was an American who had just fallen from a balloon into the African jungle.

'I t'ink I come for de opera season,' Punch said, then as if instantly realizing he was supposed to be dying, 'Watah! I'm dying, dying, dying.'

An airman in red, gold and green, he looked up at the sky and the eyes of Battle followed.

'Jesus Chris'' up dere but you won't see him. An' Abraham Lincoln down under the flo'. But whar's George Washington, dat's what Ah wants to know – '

Judy was an Ethiopian with a brass ring in her nose who approached with a whisky bottle in a convulsion of mincing jerks. 'Watah,' gasped Punch, and Judy gave him the whisky bottle. 'How you feel now? You feel better now?' 'Where am I?' 'This is Kayonka country, Africa.' 'You can't fool me.' 'It just so happens I'se de sister of de chief ob de tribe and here comes my brother now.' 'You're the chief of police?' Punch greeted the chieftain. 'Well, I was in New York myself.' 'Do you know Billy Minsky's?' 'Yes sir, and let me tell you I wish I was there now for the giant is eating all our tribe up.' 'The Giants in New York?' 'No, no baseball here.' 'I'm a college guardian myself ... '

Mr Kalowsky was getting restless. Leaning over to Plantagenet he said, 'What do they want to give us this nonsense for? They should give us humoristic stories.'

Garry was also restless. 'I'll tell you a better story than this,' he said. 'Say, will you tell him I can tell better stories than this?' he whispered, half looking at the doctor, who did not appear to have heard.

On the stage the chief was saying, 'Meet my sister,

Sakoluki,' while Punch-Caspar shook hands with the ring in her nose, to the enormous delight of Battle.

Suddenly, from the back of the stage, there was a roaring like the seaplane that had been circling the harbour, and something began slowly to rise there, over the horizon. It was the hand of the giant. Just as Punch and Judy were snatching a kiss it grabbed the chief, slowly sinking from sight again with him.

'Look, the giant got him,' Garry said.

'We should have humoristic stories,' complained Mr Kalowsky, 'not this nonsense. We should have Charlie Chaplin two times a week – he would be only too pleased to come.'

'Take dat ring out of yo' nose,' advised Battle.

'The giant's blind,' said Garry.

'Sometimes the most creative suggestions come from patients,' the doctor said to Plantagenet in an undertone. 'We often get many leads for analysis from these things.'

'Where's the giant gone?' asked Punch.

'Behind me,' said Battle, 'getting dat ole shoe shine.'

Mr Kalowsky clicked his tongue.

The hand of the blind giant rose again. Judy was captured.

As the hand plunged about reaching for Punch with a weird accelerated motion which cast glowering shadows on the wall, it struck Plantagenet that the drama was being diverted from its course by some sinister disposition of the puppeteer's; he sensed, or thought he did, the doctor's increasing discomfort, as of a god, he thought, who discovers all over again that man is not long to be trusted with the strings of his destiny. Was it only his imagination, or was the puppeteer trying to deliberately frighten them? If so, the attempt was not proving much of a success; both

Garry and Mr Kalowsky were contemptuous, and of the others only Battle was encouraging. The rest were indifferent.

Plantagenet suspected he was the only one who was frightened; nor was he frightened now so much by the hand, nor the shadows, which partook of the familiarity of his delirium, as by that fact. He had the curious feeling that he had made a sort of descent into the maelstrom, a maelstrom terrifying for the last reason one might have expected : that there was about it sometimes just this loathsome, patient calm.

My God, he thought suddenly, why *am* I here, in this doleful place? And without quite knowing how this had come about, he felt that he had voyaged downward to the foul core of his world; here was the true meaning underneath all the loud inflamed words, the squealing headlines, the arrogant years. But here too, equally, he thought, looking at the doctor, was perhaps the cure, the wisdom and vision, more patient still ... And goodness was here too – he glanced at his two friends – yes, by what miracle did it come about that compassion and love were here too?

And he wondered if the doctor ever asked himself what point there was in adjusting poor lunatics to a mischievous world over which merely more subtle lunatics exerted almost supreme hegemony, where neurotic behaviour was the rule, and there was nothing but hypocrisy to answer the flames of evil, which might be the flames of Judgment, which were already scorching nearer and nearer ... He saw that the doctor, sweat trickling down his face, leaning forward anxiously, was almost exhausted.

With this realization, his mind wandered. He began, as often before, to imagine himself abandoned. The doctor, his last hope, on his final frontier, would have no time for him, or his friends. He saw the plunging hand only as his fate, the hieroglyphic of 'they', which was seeking him out, to take him away : now he became Caspar, dodging absurdly from one side of the stage to the other; now he envisaged himself in the familiar role of one driven friendless through hostile country into ever darker corners, more remote hiding places.

The show was at an end and he did not know whether Punch had escaped or not.

'More next week,' the puppeteer said, laughing.

'If he'd got hold of him he'd been mashed potatoes by now,' Battle said, getting up, 'been skinmeat.'

'It's a lot of nonsense!' said Mr Kalowsky. 'We should have humoristic stories.'

The blinds ran up, letting in the glare; the stage was put away, the giant, Punch, Judy, the chief and the balloon laid in boxes neatly, the magic lantern telescoped into a canvas case. The doctor went off rapidly with the puppeteer, without a glance behind.

Soon, as if the patients had been merely resting on their pilgrimage, the obsequious procession round the wards was resumed. Faces that had been intent for a time, however negatively, upon the antics of Caspar, collapsed in grey misery. At first there was a little speculation about the show : then not a nod. The shuffling began all over again. An attendant, jangling his keys, shouted, 'Get up, keep moving there!' while Garry, Bill, Mr Kalowsky and even Battle walked in silence too, finally, their heads bowed like the others in that marathon of the dead. The audience had broken up, each man to his inner Africa.

VIII

Pneumatic Tube Station 382; Electro-cardiograph dept.
257. Operating Rooms 217; Physiotherapy 320; Neuro
Path. Laboratory 204; Dial O for Psychiatric numbers ...

Sometimes it was only when he read the writing on
the wall that he remembered where he was, and now,
entering the wardroom annex, he remembered. Yet
gone for a few minutes late that hot thundery after-
noon was the atmosphere of a City Hospital. There
was about the curtained scene a ghastly cosiness, a
deceptive gaiety. As he sat down to the piano and
swung into 'Sweet and Low', he was harrowed to
think how obliquely perfect an expression his rendi-
tion was of the tortured memories it might have
evoked had he been playing it straight. But he was not
playing it straight, no one could have recognized the
tune, and yet he was absurdly disappointed by the
indifference of his audience. They might have been
watching the puppet show again. He began to play
a little louder, smiling at Garry, who was leaning over
his shoulder, and at Mr Kalowsky, who was sitting
near in a wicker chair, nodding encouragement, as he
chorded into 'These Foolish Things'. His hands trem-
bled still, but their trembling was stayed now by the
vise of his determination. As he felt at the moment he
might have had no more than a medicable case of the
jitters, the kind of morning-after during which he
suffered agonies between bromides over the spectacle
he had made of himself last night; quite overlooking
the anonymity, the inconspicuous precision, even the
courtliness of his behaviour: for who had seen him,
in the deserted corridor, wander mistakenly into the

ladies' room, who had remarked that vomit placed with inimitable, circumspect painstakingness under the fire extinguisher? And then the upright journey down in the lift, the humming hotel lobby reeling under the palmettos where not an eye turned his way, and the miles on miles upon miles swimming home with the instinct of a salmon ... No, were his past just such a feeble sum of prankishness, were his past not as the nations – and which of *them* dared stop drinking, dared face the knees of the years knocking together? – did there not exist in it, quite apart from what details he accurately, remorsefully recalled of the criminal folly of his life, or the irreparable damage he had done, such a long weary heritage of unsalvageable aftermath, he might have been able to persuade himself, by his physical symptoms, that he had such a hangover, with its attendant harmless delusions, that it really 'relieved' him to imagine what his brothers would say to the game of whist Battle was conducting with two glistening Negro sailors in the centre of the annex, could it have been transferred to the drawing-room he had in mind.

'Oh Lord,' Battle caracoled, 'look at Miss Diamond there – gwine to make plenty money, bo.'

'You tellin' me.'

'Jesus it's de King ob Man,' Battle slapped down the King of Hearts, 'I break de table with dat.'

'Kill 'em!'

'Too young and he *lays* on de Jack like dat.'

'T'ank you, boss, we cleaned him up.'

'Goodbye, I'se de ace ob whist!' Battle was half singing now, but not to Bill's music. Something in the rhythm of his blood, it seemed, did not like Bill's music; not because it was alien music, it was precisely because it sounded too cognate that he would not conform to it.

Glancing sideways at Battle, Plantagenet felt the Negro was jealous of his music, that he resented it, as that poor defective behind him with the long blond hair and a hanging jaw resented it, though from an envy of a different quality. Altering his tune to '*Milneburg Joys*', he looked carelessly about him, at the patients lolling against the piano opposite Garry, out of some surviving domestic habit doubtless, since they weren't listening, at the poor defective, at the two nurses interminably, sthenically discussing an autopsy, at the closed door of the doctor's office.

'When we get out of here,' Garry whispered in Bill's ear, 'some Saturday morning I'm going to buy some rope and put it in the crabbing nets, and then get some fish heads and I'll tie them in the net, and I'll put the net on a wagon, and my lunch, and get my brother and me and we'll go down – and you'll come with us of course, and Mr Kalowsky – and we'll all go down to the dock and stay all day, and then on the way back we'll sell a couple of dozen and maybe get a dollar and then go back and cook the rest and then after we eat them and go to the show we have some sort of candy and then do the very same thing the next day.' Out of the corner of his eye Plantagenet could see Battle and the Negroes watching him with disdain as his fingers picked out the pattern of Garry's innocent day.

'I was standin' in de window one day,' Battle announced, 'when de captain and de mate dey had a few words, when dat great *Titanic struck*,' he slapped down a card.

But his song gradually assembled itself into something with a strange encompassing rhythm to which

41

the feet and hands of the other Negro card-players responded as with a soft beating of Haitian tambours:

> 'When dat great Titanic hit dat cold iceberg
> Say back up Shine and take another blow,
> I got a concrete bottom and a barfroom flo' ...'

'Yeh man,' whispered the other card-players, 'yeh man,' they drummed with their feet and hands while Battle flung down each card he played violently.

'So up jump Shine from de deck below
Says, Cap'n don' you know
Water comin' in your barfroom do'?
Say Shine, go back and pack a few mo' sacks
'Cause I got fifty-four pumps to keep dis water back ...'

Plantagenet began to strike some chords having little in common with each other save that they were minor.

'I can tell you a better song than that,' Garry whispered uneasily. 'Go on playing and I'll tell you.' He played 'In a Mist'. 'I saw a ship a-sailing, a-sailing on the sea, and oh, it was a lady with pretty things for thee, there were comforts in the cabin and apples in the hall, there were four-and-twenty white mice stood between the decks – '

> 'Say yes sir, Cap, I know dat too
> But dis one time yo' work won' do;
> So Shine went down, he began to think,
> Ah t'ink dis big boat won' sink.'

'Dis big boat won' sink,' repeated some of the others thoughtfully, cards poised.

Battle raised his card aloft and turning his eyes

ceilingward as if in benediction declared:

'Shine look up and said dese people take me fo' a fool.' Battle smacked down his card, shuffling his feet under the table.

'But Ah'm gwine to jump overboard and gwine to *Liverpool*.'

The word detached itself from the card game like a missile directed straight at Plantagenet, who abruptly changed to *'Singing the Blues'*. He played Frankie Trumbauer's old version fast.

'So Shine jumps overboard and begins to swim
So all de people on de boat were lookin' after him!'

The card-players swayed in their seats.

'Listen!' said Garry, 'I can tell you a better sea poem. Listen! We were shattered in a *cabin*; not a soul dared to stir; the storm was on the deep while the angry sea roared; and the thunder sounded like the trumpet and the lightning cut away his mast. Well, the captain staggered down the stairs and the little daughter gripped his icy hands and the father said, " 'Tis well, little daughter, for we are done." Next day we anchored in the harbour, safe.'

'Why dat de Cap'n's daughter standin' on de deck
With her drawers up around her neck
Say, come back here and save po' me
Ah'll give you a lot of dat what you want, you see,
But go back whore and get yo'self ready
You ain't no good standin' shiverin' like a cold box
jelly ... '

'Like a cold box jelly – '
'Listen! I'll tell you a better story about an iceberg. Better than that.' Garry's eyes were fixed on Bill's face. He leaned closer. 'It was late in September when

a large whaling boat headed north going to catch whales in the cold seas – ' Plantagenet was becoming so nervous he kept putting his hand to his mouth thinking he had a cigarette in it; once he even leaned out for an imaginary cigarette consuming itself in an imaginary tray, but *'Singing the Blues'* rattled on like some combustion engine he had set in motion. ' – and in the bay one of the men spotted this black whale – ' 'Are you sure it wasn't a white whale,' he asked. He fumbled a break, recovered and went on. 'It was a black whale all right, whales are black, not white.'

He was playing with furious quiet now, *'Fierce Raged the Tempest O'er the Deep'.*

'And dere was de Cap'n standin' on de deck
He say come back here and save po' me
I'll make you richer dan any shine should be ...
But Shine had his head in a gap
And his tail in a swing
Dis is one time dese ol' people
Can't tell Shine a thing ... '

' – well, so they stuck the harpoon inside the whale and the whale went along and smashed into the iceberg and it was killed and they hauled him up and tied it alongside and they salted it and packed it in the barrels until there was only bones.'

'And the iceberg,'

'That was all broken, smashed.'

'Say dis ole sun going' down and dis ole water gettin'
  cool
Ah got to shake a wicked tail to get to Liverpool – '

'Say, look here, all you people! God don! Ah gonna hippertize him! Ah gonna hippertize you!' Battle shouted. He got up, scattering the cards on the floor.

'Go on playing, go on playing, please!' Garry said, and he softly played the *'Death of Ase'* for him in ragtime, with his right hand in the base.

'Listen, wherever I am I can tell a story. No matter where you put me, even in prison. Will you tell the doctor I can tell them?'

Battle and the other Negroes gathered round the piano, elbowing aside the patients lolling there. Glancing at Battle for approval, Plantagenet struck four jagged chords, one for the death of Ase, one for the doom of the *Titanic*, one for the *Pequod*, one for the whale, white or black it didn't matter which. Battle eyed him stonily. Plantagenet struck up *'Clarinet Marmalade'*. He was playing wonderfully well, he thought.

'Say listen,' Battle demanded, 'let's have some truckin' – don't you know any truckin','

'Very nice,' said Mr Kalowsky encouragingly. 'Now give us some humoristic music.'

Suddenly the defective got up. 'You don't know nohing, you souse,' he said, pushing him. 'Lemme at that piano.'

'Yeah, yuh give us truckin',' said Battle.

Plantagenet vacated his seat for the defective, who immediately began to play.

'Huh hum! Doom doom!' boomed the Negroes, cheering and stomping: the lolling patients took up a cawing: 'Tee da, do; aw-aw, de pupdebup, da; wooh!'

Battle started to signal in time to the music. 'Move yo' han' to E. Wen you' do make M yo' do move to F.'

The little man with a beard, passing, said to himself loudly, 'That's semaphore, all Boy Scouts use it.'

Plantagenet was holding his trembling hands out before him, fascinated, though none save Garry and

Mr Kalowsky appeared to be paying any attention,
when he saw the doctor beckoning from the open door
of his office.

> *'All you good peoples come on down to me.*
> *So de debbil turned over in hell*
> *And began to laugh and grin*
> *Say, yo' took a mighty long time comin', Shine,*
> *But yo' welcome in!'*

IX

'Come in,' said Doctor Claggart gravely, letting him
pass through the door first. The doctor, in a white
robe, seemed to people the room with phantoms. An
electric fan was droning with multitudinous
monotony. 'Now,' said Doctor Claggart, still behind
him, 'it seems that you can't stay here as a public
charge, since you're a foreigner.'

'I – what,' said Plantagenet, looking round him, be-
wildered. He couldn't find the doctor among the
phantoms, for the curtains, blowing in at that
moment, made one whiteness with his robe. A chill
had entered. Though still bemused by the incident at
the piano, and sweating with the heat, he felt it touch
his spine.

'And I don't suppose you want to pay five dollars a
day *to* stay here.'

Next door a typewriter rattled and stopped. He
found the doctor, seated opposite him, at his desk.

'I've arranged for you to stay the night, but you'll
have to leave in the morning.'

A drop of sweat fell from Plantagenet's forehead to
his toe. After a moment he said : 'Things are going too

fast for me. I don't want to go just yet. I knew I could of course, though.'

'Yes. It's far too soon of course. Pity. I'd like to help you, if I could – you're an interesting case.'

'There are so many things I wanted to talk to you about – '

'You might begin by telling me your real name. First you said Lawhill, and that's the name we booked you by. Then you said Plantagenet. Plantagenet!'

The man in the dirty robe stared back at the doctor mutely, his eyes blank.

'Can't remember? Or don't want to? First you thought you were a ship. and then a jazz band, or you played in a band, is this so? ... Well, feel any craving for liquor?'

'I want food more ... I missed my supper last night because your snaggle-toothed horny-faced so-and-so of a Head Nurse – excuse me – '

'I've – we've heard all about that.'

'Do you think it is excusable?'

'What do you think?'

'There are always two sides, nicht wahr, Herr Doktor, to a show like this? My side is this. At four p.m. sixteen or so of those whom you call nuts in my, sorry, in *your* ward, were taken up to play baseball on the roof – now don't think I don't appreciate that, just as I appreciated hydrotherapy et al, the old man screaming for mercy under the needle shower reminded me of stories of George III – then there was the view of the men screening sand outside, and the rubber tree that really seemed to be *enjoying* the atmosphere in the locker room! – and on the roof there was a big hot wind and a particularly nice view of the river sparking like, shall we say, glass – '

'A glass of what?'

' – well, we played anyhow, and as some people refused to go out I never went to bat – even if I'd known how to play your American game, which I do not – but I certainly enjoyed it as much as those fielders who just played imaginary twirly-whirly-trill picking the grey threads out of their gowns. Be that as it may, the idea is, these gowns were the garments we had to sleep in, though at the time I hadn't realized it.'

'Don't forget it's the City Hospital.'

'Well yes ... But – it being difficult also to play in our stringless canvas shoes, most of us went barefoot and what with the heat and all we became damned dirty. I was also very jittery, but not too jittery to notice, after the excitement was over and we were being sweatily herded back, how each patient dropped back into his own world again, how senses that had thrilled to the game quickly became numbed to stupor. It isn't difficult to see, therefore, why these should conform to the routine of the hospital, should do what they were told – since they waited to be told everything – even if that happened to be not to dare to take a shower before supper at all, or even, like the disciples, to wash their feet.'

'Is that what they were told?'

'A couple of more or less sane fellows, that old paranoic Swede and the other fellow who thinks he's falling apart since a Sanitube froze on him last winter – the same fellow whose name you forgot – and that's another thing I want to talk to you about – managed to throw some water on themselves in a perfectly good bathroom upstairs adjacent to the roof entrance while we were waiting for the elevator; but they were pulled out by attendants before they had finished. They dried themselves on their gowns, in which they

48

had to sleep, like those in which we all had to sleep, are still sleeping for that matter, this is the same gown now – I wore it then and you will no doubt bury us all in them. Well, the others, including myself, just stood there sweating in the all-time high, that same all-time high that felled one hundred and eighty-six people out in the sane world, in this city.'

'The "so-called" sane world, I suppose you think? Here. Have a cigarette.'

He took the cigarette with shaking hand, feeling the doctor's eyes on him. 'Thank you,' he said slowly. 'You're not a bad chap, you know, but – ' He inhaled deeply and the room, the whiteness, spun around him with a jagged dazzle; he closed his eyes a second: where was he? what was he saying? 'Oh yes. When we got back to our floor the others, who hadn't been playing, were eating their supper. Four or five of our crowd, including Garry and, believe it or not, Battle – who, having been a ship's fireman still remembers days of comparative cleanliness – made for the bathroom, but they were pulled back by Mrs Horncle or whoever, that paranoid Head Nurse whom I have never, never seen smile at anyone save only you, dear Doctor.'

'She does her best.'

'She reminds me of an old nanny of mine, the first one I ever had, she ended up in an asylum too, she used to beat me with bramble sticks when I was five years old – '

'Those are a couple of fine give-aways you've just made.'

' – and I asked the male nurse, a sympathetic egg, who gets his carfare from giving blood for transfusions, poor devil, if I could have a wash. He nodded but said to step on it though ... Then, as I was preparing to step – '

'Wait a moment now, you said the others were pulled back and accepted the thing, they took it, in other words, but you wouldn't. That's one of the things I'd like to get at, Lawhill – '

'Don't call me – the *Lawhill* was a windjammer that survived more disasters than any ship afloat.'

'Oh? That's interesting.' He made a note. 'It may have been inconvenient but you could have conformed, as the others did – '

'– Nurse who said: "Come back here. If you're going to wash you must go without your supper." I said: "Right. To hell with supper then," and – '

'In effect that's what you've said all your life.'

'I ran round to the bathroom and threw some water on my face, but there was nothing to dry on. So I went to my bed, took the sheet off and was drying myself on that when Mrs H. suddenly rose up before me breathing fire.'

'And what did Mrs H., as you call her, say to you then?'

'She said: "Your conduct is going straight to the office. You're going to pay for this. You're just a conceited Englishman, a back-alley drunk who thinks himself superior et cetera, et cetera." She said an inspection had to be made later, and "Don't you know everything has to *look* neat in the hospital? *You're going to suffer for this.*" I said the sheet was no worse than it was before, they're all filthy anyway.'

'Yes,' said Dr Claggart. 'All of them are, I'm afraid. It's the City Hospital.' The buzzer on his desk rang and he rose and went off whitely.

Plantagenet walked over to the window behind Claggart's desk. The glass tower, he thought. Pulling

consciousness. Strange, he hadn't noticed before that this park was here at all. How lovely it was! The feeling of storm communicated itself to him; he drew a deep breath – outside there was life, with all its infinite poignancy. A little children's fountain had sent up a rainbow, an outspread peacock's fan of water, whose coolness could almost be felt, and for a moment connecting this with rain falling somewhere already, something like a hope flickered in him, though of nothing in particular, perhaps just of hope itself. But of course it was the fountain, not the rain, that made the rainbow : his hope was a false hope, an artificial one. By the time the rain really came, bringing relief to the drought, the sun would be set, just as it might happen that by the time madness came to a man, the mind would not know it was a relief.

There was a rumble of thunder; the sleepers, who had been lying down there as the dead might lie, resting for a while in some green niche of Paradise, he thought, or in a no-man's-land between two worlds of light and dark, began to stir, stretching themselves. The leaves and buds were dropping faster now, falling straight like rain, and now, in the gathering darkness, they were like ghosts of leaves or buds, or truly rain. There was an urgent note, suddenly, in the cries of children : a pigeon whirred up in a silver panic, making a short parabola : one leaf was spinning, another spiralled downwards, squirrels scattered. Again he took two steps towards the ward, again he returned to the window. As he watched those yellow buds like rain, or little flowers, he was filled again with his old persistent sorrow, and sorrow now for his two friends. The cries of children, the falling leaves, the lovers who were now running for shelter, laughing, their arms round one another – what part had all these in their stricken lives? Even the riven trees, yearning into the gloom, lit now by the heliotrope of lightning, still felt their roots in the true earth, their crests in the sky, at least they could speak to each other according to the special reality of their existence, they sensed where they were going, or what they had become; when their leaves fell they were aware also that that was what must be, it was right. Now their branches nodded, the nameless trees were nodding to each other; he could hear the rustling of leaves, or of water falling on leaves. The deepest sleepers were awake, drawing their coats around them.

But one ragged man sat motionless under a tree watching, as though he knew the storm as the trees knew it; Plantagenet wondered if he had ever been such a one, to whom a lost moment of tempest was a lost moment with God. Far above him a young girl with a white collar was leaning under a blue sunblind which suddenly bellied like a sail. Far below, the leaves were blowing towards the solitary man, an army viewed from a mountain top, advancing over the plain.

Perhaps this solitary man, perhaps this young girl, were the very ones who would yet lead his friends out of their bondage? Perhaps, but he would never know.

Then the evening storm broke in earnest. Aloft, a thousand striped sunblinds were set dancing; through the drunkard's rigadoon of the raindrops, through the black park, white mariners were luminously gliding.

He moved over to another window where he could see the river below: it was sparkling like ginger ale; now it seethed with a million sequins. A lull came. The rain lifted, though a few large drops still fell:

under the lowering sky the river was very swift. Looking down at it a delicious sense of freedom possessed him, a sense of being already outside, free to run with the wind if he wished, free to run as far away from the hospital as he liked. Yet the bars were still there, and they resembled the bars of his mind, set by the cause of his presence at all in this place. He had not escaped them yet, nor would he escape them merely by leaving. His thoughts flowed past with the rain-swollen river, but his thoughts did not escape either, they contracted always to the point from which he was watching, the hospital itself. And he understood obscurely that what he'd said to the doctor about Garry was true: the boy had become a part of himself, as had Mr Kalowsky, a part of the shadowy meaning of his destiny. He pressed his face against the bars ... *à fuir, là-bas!*

Where were all the good honest ships tonight, he wondered, bound for all over the world? Lately it had seemed to him they passed more rarely. Only nightmare ships were left in this stream. All at once, watching the strange traffic upon it, he fancied that the East River was as delirious, as haunted as the minds that brooded over it, it was a mad river of grotesque mastless steamers, of flat barges slipping along silent as water snakes, a river of railroad boats the shape of army tanks with their askew funnels appearing to have been built on to outriggers, or they were strange half-ships, preposterously high out of the water with naked propellers thrashing like tuna fish, with single masts out of alignment. This world of the river was one where everything was uncompleted while functioning in degeneration, from which as from Garry's barge, the image of their own shattered or unformed souls was cast back at them. Yes, it was as if all complementary factors had been with-drawn from this world! Its half-darkness quivered with the anguish of separation from the real light; just as in his nightmare, the tortoise crawled in agony looking for its shell, and nails hammered held nothing together, or one-winged birds dropped exhausted across a maniacal, sunless moon ...

He started as though someone had touched him on the shoulder. Nobody. But Doctor Claggart, his hand on the polished knob of the open door of his office, was watching him from a distance with eyes which said plainly: 'Get back to the ward.' He had gone.

The piano was still open; Plantagenet shut it care-fully. Then he started reluctantly. Electric numbers twinkled on a board before him: '7', '11', '7', '11'. The deserted corridor, where he had so often walked with Garry and Mr Kalowsky, seemed queerly beauti-ful to him this evening under the dust. The last stormy light cast its curdling brightness in the reflected steel prison bars at the foot of the far bed. As he linger-ingly approached the room facing the wharves there was another savage scribble of lightning across the windows, from which some of the patients were mov-ing away. Others were laughing nervously, though Garry and Mr Kalowsky were in their usual places, waiting for him. He joined them without a word. No attendants seemed to be about. There was a perplex-ing silence.

'Did you tell the doctor I was sane?' asked Mr Kalowsky at length, cheerfully.

He nodded. 'We're all going to be O.K.'

The old man looked at him sharply.

'That's keen,' Garry said. 'Do you think I can get out soon? But I don't care. All I want is to tell stories. I've got a story for you now.' His eyes strayed to the

66

familiar old barge lying below them. 'Well, I went down to the beach and I met two of my friends. We went on this rotten old barge full of mud and sand and a lot of junk. We were playing follow the leader and I got dizzy. I climbed out. I looked all right, I was small. When I got home my mother threw me in the tub and I got some clean clothes on. Yes sir. A few years later the barge fell apart.

'It was all collapsed,' he added, as thunder rocked the hospital. The rain started to souse down again from the eaves.

'You will only get worser here, what are you here for? What's the matter with your head, Garry,' Mr Kalowsky said sternly but kindly, as thunder shook the building again. 'Put something in your stomach, otherwise you won't last it. Look at you! Look at this hospital full of lunatics half starved with hunger, they go crazy – look at them – and they all come clopping to the hospitals.' He pointed to a poor trembling old man running by with a grey shawl over his shoulders and Plantagenet remembered how whenever you spoke to him he drew it over his head with fright. 'Your stomach's going on the revolution. Wake up, you brains! Brains of the world unite! My experience in the hospital is that the workers are against us more than the capitalists. I don't believe in God. I talk too much Bob Ingersoll wisdom and that's why Police Megoff wants to lock me up. Jesus Christ! If the workers will wake up and buy brains I won't need to go to the hospital! Give the patients nicer to eat! Listen, once they pulled three teeth out of me, out of my mouth. That's the capitalist system. I should have knocked the three teeth out of him.' There was a flash of lightning, a man screamed. 'Anyway,' Mr Kalowsky added, 'these young fellows who say I am in my second childhood should go home and clean their diapers. Whether I go or not – '

There was another lull in this twilight storm and in the silence the rain could be heard hissing in the river. Some of the patients who had been frightened were returning to the room. The moon had risen over a ragged tantivy of clouds; an oil barge was passing, her tiny contiguous funnels pillowed by tanks; following her was a dredger, to which a float many fathoms to starboard was attached in a remote, umbilical way. After her, at some distance, a Fall River sidewheeler was steaming close inshore. Fall River! How delighted Ruth had been that day long ago because they had a cabin on the top deck of the *Providence*! It was his first day in New York, summer then too, and they had paced the deck arm in arm. In the evening they had wandered around the ancient, lacquered ship, like a vast London hotel with its gilt stairways. From the muffled corridor they saw the firemen shovelling, down below. They had listened together to that pulse of the ship he could hear now. What had they not learned about the world and each other in that cabin so high up in the ship? They had not learned that with all the beauty of the evening, the softness of the night, the tenderness of the blue morning, that every beat of the engine which took them nearer to New Bedford, nearer to Herman Melville, was also taking them nearer to their own white whale, their own destruction.

The thunder started again. The sidewheeler was much closer now, her paddles lashing the spasmodically stormlit water into a creamy foam. All at once, as if an anguished desire to teach her, to touch her before she was gone, had spontaneously seized them, three gesticulating Negro sailors rushed to the bars:

68

climbing up within the steel meshes they started a roaring which was instantly taken up by almost everyone in the ward. Was the ship the *Providence* herself? He couldn't be sure. But he stood, transfixed with anguish, watching her go. The roaring had become an uncontrollable yell by now, the Negroes were beating on the bars, shaking the windows. He remembered his freighter with the cargo of animals: there had been not only lions but elephants, tigers, jaguars, all bound for a zoo. The panthers died, in the Indian Ocean at night the lions roared, the elephants trumpeted and vomited so that none save the carpenter dared go forward: when they smashed into the hurricane the jaguars moaned in terror like frightened children. No forest had ever plunged so deeply in the long bending winds as that ship, while 'Let us out, let us be free,' was the meaning of that wailing during these bitter hours. He had thought, 'Let us be free to suffer like animals.' And that cry was perhaps more human than the one he now heard. The lightning had become so nearly continuous that the heavens seemed to be full of flaming trees and icebergs. The moon had gone. A forked tree of light shot up diagonally. Somewhere there was the long hiss of shattering glass. An iceberg hurled northward through the clouds and as it poised in its onrush, tilted, he saw his dream of New York crystallized there for an instant, glittering, illuminated by a celestial brilliance, only to be reclaimed by dark, by the pandemonium of an avalanche of falling coal which, mingling with the cries of the insane speeding the *Providence* on her way, coalesced in his brain with what it conjured of the whole mechanic calamity of the rocking city, with the screaming of suicides, of girls tortured in hotels for transients, of people burning to death in vice dens, through all of which a thousand ambulances were screeching like trumpets.

Then the ship had gone, the excitement subsided. The patients drifted away from the window, keys clanked, the attendants were arriving to lay the table for supper of the poor old men who were considered too disgusting to eat with the others.

'We can only wait and see. So many things can happen in a lifetime,' said Mr Kalowsky calmly, as they turned from the window.

Garry caught Plantagenet by the sleeve of his soiled dressing-gown. 'You haven't said one word,' he said.

'There was too much noise.'

'They want to smash our friendship, isn't that it?' Garry said. 'Isn't that what the doctor told you? It is condemned.'

He shook his head. 'Of course not, Garry. We're all O.K.'

'You can't fool me; they don't want me to tell you anything more. No more stories, nothing. They aren't going to let us out. Tomorrow maybe they're going to put me in another ward. All right, let them try. They won't break us. The world won't let anything good be.' After a moment he said absently, 'Look at Mr Battle.'

Battle was now semaphoring by the window at the night. 'Ayeh, Beah, Gee,' he was saying. 'To make X yuh do AX den yuh make D with an H and that's H, no sah!' Only the vast heliograph of the lightning responded distantly.

Plantagenet drifted back to the window, from which Battle had departed. It was clearing up; there were fluctuant sable pools on the wharves. Concertinas of orange and green lights quivered in their depths. Scattered wild steam rose from the gratings by the powerhouse. He could see the moon reeling through the sky taking refuge from time to time in clouds, as does a man in saloons, but she was never quite hidden from sight. Soon her insane light fell on the wet grass where the hospital lights were now reflected. The grass was very green and the sparrows hopped among little white skulls of clover lying among its narrow blades. Mr Kalowsky nudged him, he turned.

The nine high electric candles in their hollow circular base were lit above the poor old men who were having their dinner.

A seaplane was gliding whitely past, and now it was turning, to Plantagenet suddenly it had the fins and flukes and blunt luminous head of a whale; now it roared straight at the window, straight at *him*.

A bell was ringing shockingly somewhere, keys were rattling, and there was the slop-slop-slop of feet in the corridor. Battle was signalling again; without purpose or need or hope he signalled at the night, at the approaching seaplane : 'A, B, C, D – '

' – to make H you do make AX and den you make D with A and that's H – no sah!'

Something extraordinary was happening to him, he tried to struggle with the words, with whatever it was that was going on, to struggle with this maniacal force which was – which was changing him, for that was it, he was changing – '

'I was dizzy,' Mr Kalowsky said. 'I lay down, 'tis not the gutter, 'tis more like a trench here where I took a schnooze.'

Garry joined them at the window.

'It only looks like spring,' Garry was saying slowly, 'and it's summer. It takes such a long time to grow. It looks as though it's only spring, when the grass is just sprouting up, it's so small, and the clover's growing slow, the dandelions are not out quite, but they will be, yes sir, and look, there's a path running through the little grass hill. It only looks like spring, that's all.'

There was a furious crash of thunder and simultaneously Plantagenet felt the impact of the plane, the whale, upon his mind. While metamorphosis nudged metamorphosis, a kind of order, still preserved within his consciousness, and enclosing this catastrophe, exploded itself into the age of Kalowsky again, and into the youth of Garry, who both now seemed to be spiralling away from him until they were lost, just as the seaplane was actually tilting away, swaying up to the smashed sky. But while that part of him only a moment before in possession of the whole, the ship, was turning over with disunion of hull and masts uprooted falling across her decks, another faction of his soul, relative to the ship but aware of these fantasies and simultanities as it were from above, knew him to be screaming against the renewed thunder and saw the attendants closing in on him, yet saw him too, as the plane seethed away northwards like the disembodied shape of the very act of darkness itself, passing beyond the asylum walls melting like wax, and following in its wake, sailing on beyond the cold coast of the houses and the factory chimneys waving farewell – farewell –

XI

Once more a man paused outside the City Hospital. Once more, with a dithering crack, the hospital door had shut behind him.

Outside, he felt no sense of release, only inquietude. He kept gazing back with a sort of longing at the building that had been his home. It was really rather beautiful, he felt, turning at a corner store.

Here he bought a packet of stamps with little reproductions of tigers on them from the Straits Settlements, and elephants from India : a Negro climbed a tree on a Senegalese variety, there was a duck-billed platypus from Australia, another more terrible sort of tiger, from Obangui-Tchaeri-Tchad.

He had thought of sending these up to Garry but instead he pocketed them himself with a queer cancelled feeling. It was too hard to return to the hospital. Then such a feeling of absolute tragedy possessed him at leaving his friends behind that he conquered his fear, and retraced his steps, buying a dollar's worth of oranges on the way. At the hospital again he found a nurse and had the oranges and the stamps sent up to the observation ward for Mr Kalowsky and Garry.

Approaching midtown he began to hear strange noises, the faces of the patients were swarming about him, once he jumped nervously, imagining that Ruth was just behind. The face of Mr Battle, grinning, swooped up at him. Once he thought he saw his parents curtsying down the street with pained, terrified looks. He ran after them for half a block but they turned mysteriously into two small Indians. A member of his band disappeared into a music shop. He crossed the street. Now every stern face he encountered was that of an Immigration inspector, dogging him. After some hesitation, he threw away the bottle of whisky he had.

This had been simply, without any irony, returned to him by the janitor as his property. 'You won't be using that any more, pal,' the janitor had said.

'Thanks,' he had replied, 'I'll throw it away myself.'

So now he threw it away, into the ashcan. Then he went back and got it.

He was keeping an eye out for Melville's house, this must be the site, though all he could find was a shop, Zimmerman, carpenter, with next door a humble Spanish restaurant, d'Alarçon, proprietor. Strange, he said. He entered a church he knew, gazing about him. In the painting above, Christ was being offered a drink; he stood a while in meditation. The thought even of vinegar sent the blood coursing through his veins. There was only one other person there, a woman in black, kneeling. Here was his opportunity. When so much suffering existed, what else could a man do? With a guilty, flurried, yet triumphant motion he took a long draught of whisky. Replacing the bottle under his coat tails he hurried out.

He was elated now, feeling the fire of the whisky. Nevertheless he shunned the lovers walking by in the wind. Later he followed two more lovers, sure the girl with the silver fox fur was Ruth. Suddenly they vanished.

Signs along the street mocked at him : *Business as usual during alterations: Broken Blossoms: Dead End: No cover at any time. World's loveliest girls. Larger, more modern.* He waved them aside.

In the subway, the roar of the train seemed to be trying to communicate with him. First it said 'womb', then 'tomb'. Then it said both in succession, very rapidly, over and over again.

Above ground, under the El, he paused in the dappled sunlight swept by enormous shadows. Here he took another drink. This was like a forest; out of the forest had grown the church, from the church, the ship. So he had learned : but soon they would

74

scrap the El, soon there would be nothing at all : no ship, no church, no forest, no shadows, no learning. It would all be collapsed, as Garry would have said.

Stepping out of the sunlight he turned unconsciously towards the waterfront. At the corners of streets loomed up the deathly white of hamburger stands : *Whale steaks 5c*. There was a smell of ropes here, of seafaring, and strange merchandise, a smell he knew well, but which hurt, like the smell of women's furs in the rain.

His footsteps took him to the sailors' tavern he knew, a bad spot. He ordered a whisky and sat down in a corner. Here was no one : no lunatics to jeer at him, no sane people to encourage or exhort him, not even a piano this time, only the world of ghosts coming closer, but in order that it might not come too close, always another drink; he was having a hell of a good time. He began to think he saw some of his mistakes clearly. He had them all figured out. He even imagined himself expunging them by some heroic sacrifice, that would not only justify him to Garry and Mr Kalowsky, but would, in a fantastic sense, free them. Free them? It would free everyone – all the patients, all the parents, all the Ruths, it would free mankind; ah – he would strike his blow for the right.

Ennobled, he went to the washroom where he finished his bottle. Glancing round for somewhere to put it he noticed an obscene sketch of a girl chalked on the wall. For some reason, suddenly enraged, he hurled the bottle against this drawing, and in the instant he drew back to escape the fragments of glass, it seemed to him that he had flung that bottle against all the indecency, the cruelty, the hideousness, the filth and injustice in the world. At the same time an atrocious vision of Garry flashed across his consciousness, and an atrocious fear. 'It was only a little scratch,' he had said.

It was dark, the darkness was full of vibrations. That terrible old woman he had seen posting the letter, was it she who was with him at the bottom of some mine?

Returning to the saloon he picked out a secluded place to sit, where they brought his whisky.

But feeling he was being watched, even there, he moved later, drink in hand, to the very obscurest corner of the bar, where, curled up like an embryo, he could not be seen at all.